My "c" Sound Box®

WRITTEN BY JANE BELK MONCURE • ILLUSTRATED BY REBECCA THORNBURGH

The Child's World®
childsworld.com

Published by The Child's World®
1980 Lookout Drive • Mankato, MN 56003-1705
800-599-READ • www.childsworld.com

ISBN HARDCOVER: 9781503823068
ISBN PAPERBACK: 9781503831285
LCCN: 2017960287

Printed in the United States of America
PA02371

A NOTE TO PARENTS AND EDUCATORS:

Magic moon machines and five fat frogs are just a few of the fun things you can share with children by reading books with them. Reading aloud helps children in so many ways! It introduces them to new words, motivates them to develop their own reading skills, and expands their attention span and listening abilities. So it's important to find time each day to share a book or two . . . or three!

As you read with young children, you can help develop their understanding of how print works by talking about the parts of the book—the cover, the title, the illustrations, and the words that tell the story. As you read, use your finger to point to each word, modeling a gentle sweep from left to right.

Simple word games help develop important prereading skills, including an understanding of rhyme and alliteration (when words share the same beginning sound, such as "six" and "sand"). Try playing with words from a book you've just shared: "What other words start with the same sound as moon?" "Cat and hat, do those words rhyme?" The possibilities are endless—and so are the rewards!

My "c" Sound Box®

This book uses the hard "c" sound in the story line. Blends are included. Words beginning with the soft "c" sound and the "ch" sound are included at the end of the book.

Little 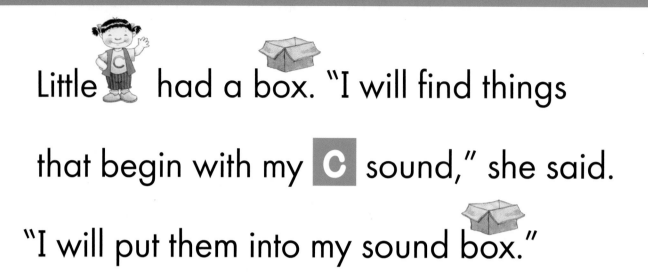 had a box. "I will find things that begin with my C sound," she said.

"I will put them into my sound box."

Little  was cold. She found some coats. Little put on a coat.

Did she put the other coats 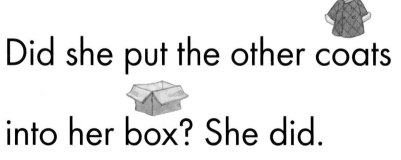 into her box? She did.

Little found some caps.

She put on a cap.

Did she put the other caps into her box with the coats? She did.

Then Little  saw a caterpillar.

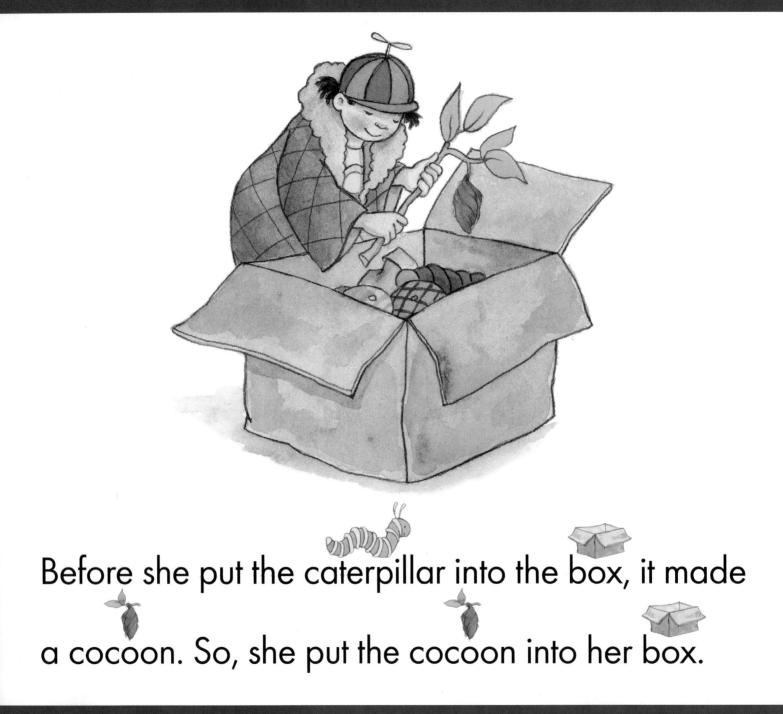

Before she put the caterpillar into the box, it made

a cocoon. So, she put the cocoon into her box.

Soon Little  found a car. She got into the

car and went for a drive in the country.

She saw a cat. The cat was chasing a canary.

Little  caught the cat. She put it into her box.

Then she called to the canary. The canary flew into a cage. Little put the cage and the canary into her box.

Little  saw a cow and a calf near a field of corn. She put the cow, the calf, and some corn into her box.

The Little drove her car through a desert. She saw a camel and a cactus. She put them into her box.

She drove to the end of a road.

She found a castle! A big castle.

A clown was at the castle door. "Come in," said the clown.

Little got out of the car. She

carried her box into the castle.

She saw candy canes, cookies,

and a cake with candles on it.

"You are just in time for my party!" said the clown.

Little  took off her coat and cap.

She lifted the cage with the canary out of the box. She lifted out the cocoon with the caterpillar inside.

Then all the other animals came out of the box.

They all sat down to a birthday party.

The caterpillar did not eat,

because it was still in the cocoon.

Little C's Word List

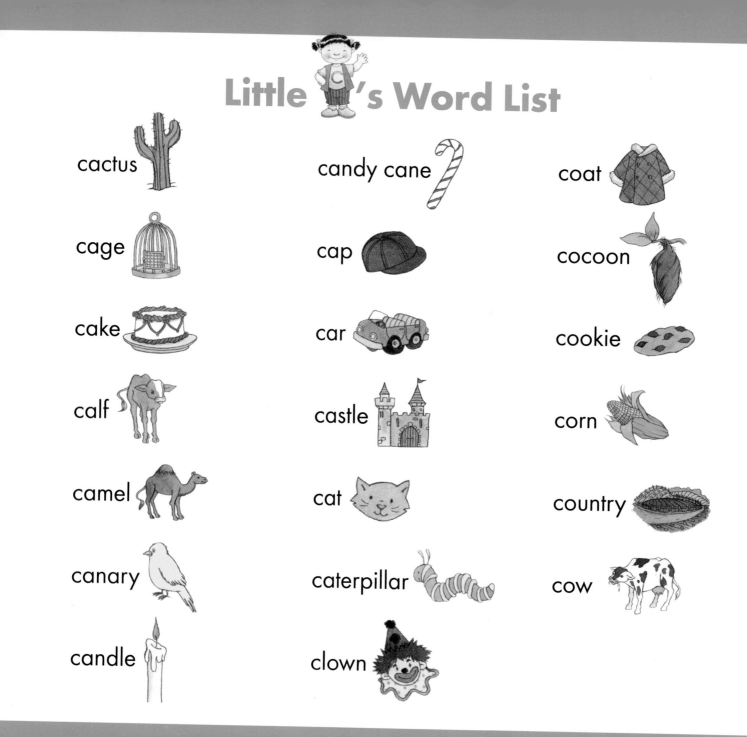

cactus

cage

cake

calf

camel

canary

candle

candy cane

cap

car

castle

cat

caterpillar

clown

coat

cocoon

cookie

corn

country

cow

Other Words with the Hard C Sound

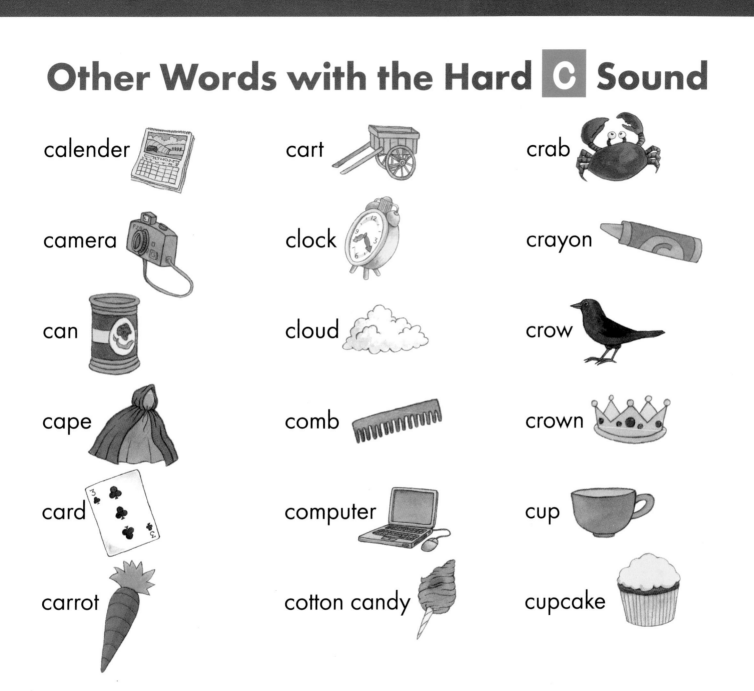

calender

camera

can

cape

card

carrot

cart

clock

cloud

comb

computer

cotton candy

crab

crayon

crow

crown

cup

cupcake

Words with the Soft C Sound

In this story, Little "c" has a hard sound—like the sound of the letter "k." Little "c" has a soft sound, too. The soft sound is like the sound of the letter "s." Read these words with Little "c," and listen for the soft sounds.

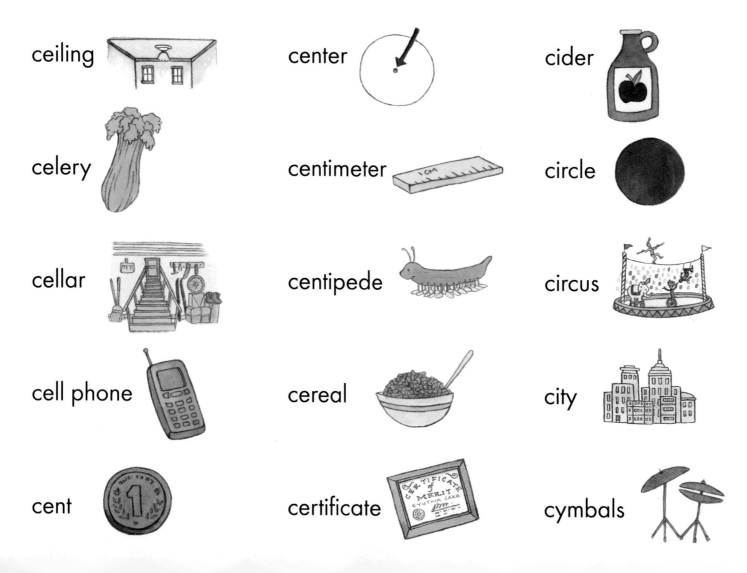

ceiling

celery

cellar

cell phone

cent

center

centimeter

centipede

cereal

certificate

cider

circle

circus

city

cymbals

Words with the ch Sound

Little "c" can get together with the letter "h" to make still another sound. Can you read these words with the "ch" sound?

chain

chart

chimney

chair

checkers

chimpanzee

chalk

cheek

chipmunk

chalkboard

cherry

chocolate

chariot

chicken

church

More to Do!

Little [clown] found a clown in a castle. The clown was having a party. He served candy canes, cookies, and a cake with candles.

You can create your own clown cupcake! Be sure an adult helps you.

Ingredients:

- 1 frosted cupcake
- 2 candy canes
- 2 chocolate chips
- 1 thin piece of red licorice
- 1 small gumdrop
- 1 sugar cone
- a little shredded coconut
- food coloring (any color)

Directions:

1. Put the coconut in a small plastic bag. Add a few drops of the food coloring. Mix the coconut until the color changes.

2. Sprinkle some of the colored coconut along the top edge of the cupcake to give your clown funny hair.

3. Use the chocolate chips for eyes and the gumdrop for the nose. Use the licorice to make a smile. Carefully break off the top parts of the candy canes to make your clown's ears.

4. Place the sugar cone on the clown's head as a hat. Now your clown cupcake is ready to make you smile twice—once when you see it and again when you eat it!

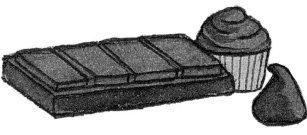

About the Author

Best-selling author Jane Belk Moncure (1926–2013) wrote more than 300 books throughout her teaching and writing career. After earning a master's degree in early childhood education from Columbia University, she became one of the pioneers in that field. In 1956, she helped form the Virginia Association for Early Childhood Education, which established the first statewide standards for teachers of young children.

Inspired by her work in the classroom, Mrs. Moncure's books became standards in primary education, and her name was recognized across the country. Her success was reflected not only in her books' popularity with parents, children, and educators, but also by numerous awards, including the 1984 C. S. Lewis Gold Medal Award.

About the Illustrator

Rebecca Thornburgh lives in a pleasantly spooky old house in Philadelphia. If she's not at her drawing table, she's reading—or singing with her band, called Reckless Amateurs. Rebecca has one husband, two daughters, and two silly dogs.